The Haunted House Mystery

THE BOBBSEY TWINS®

THE HAUNTED HOUSE MYSTERY

Laura Lee Hope

Illustrated by John Speirs

WANDERER BOOKS
Published by
Simon & Schuster, Inc., New York

Copyright © 1985 by Simon & Schuster, Inc.
Published by WANDERER BOOKS
A Division of Simon & Schuster, Inc.
Simon & Schuster Building
1230 Avenue of the Americas
New York, New York 10020

Manufactured in the United States of America
10 9 8 7 6 5 4 3 2 1

WANDERER and colophon are registered trademarks
of Simon & Schuster, Inc.

THE BOBBSEY TWINS is a trademark of Simon & Schuster, Inc.
registered in the United States Patent and Trademark Office.

Library of Congress Cataloging in Publication Data

Hope, Laura Lee.
The haunted house mystery.

(The Bobbsey twins; 12)
Summary: The Bobbsey twins suspect that odd events
at a historic Oklahoma mansion and the theft of a
duplicate dollhouse may be connected with rare animals
being stolen from the zoo.
1. Children's stories, American. [1. Twins—Fiction.
2. Oklahoma—Fiction. 3. Mystery and detective stories]
I. Speirs, John, ill. II. Title. III. Series: Hope,
Laura Lee. Bobbsey twins (1980–   ); 12.
PZ7.H772Hau 1985   [Fic]   84-25675
ISBN 0-671-54996-0

Contents

·1·

Trouble at the Airport

The big jet carrying the entire Bobbsey family taxied up to the terminal of Will Rogers World Airport in Oklahoma City, Oklahoma. Six-year-old Flossie stared out the window at the wide, flat land that surrounded them.

"Where are the cowboys and Indians?" she asked.

Her twin brother, Freddie, sat beside her with wide eyes. "I don't know," he said. "I don't even see a teepee."

Mrs. Bobbsey poked her head over the seat and smiled. "I think you'll be surprised to find Oklahoma City is just like any other city," she said.

"No registrations?" Flossie asked.

"That's reservations," Mr. Bobbsey replied from beside his wife. "We'll have reservations, all right. Hotel reservations, not Indian reservations!"

The plane stopped moving and the family stood up to leave. Dark-haired Bert and Nan, who were twelve, took their younger brother and sister by the hand so they would not get lost.

A brand-new camera hung around Freddie's neck.

Flossie tightly held a tiny dollhouse in her free hand. It was part of a prize she had won for naming the country's largest dollhouse. The trip to Oklahoma City for the unveiling was the other part of the prize.

A tall, dark-haired man in a tan suit was waiting for them in the terminal. "You must be the Bobbseys," he said. "I've been sent to meet you."

Mr. Bobbsey shook his hand. "I thought that Mrs. Wooley was going to meet us."

"She couldn't make it," the man said, and looked at Flossie's dollhouse. "I'm afraid I'm going to have to take that. It was sent to you by mistake."

"No!" Flossie said. "They gave it to me."

The man reached for the house, a large frown on his face. "We'll give you something else."

Flossie's eyes filled with tears. She had grown to love the miniature Victorian mansion, an exact duplicate of the huge dollhouse she had named.

Bert came to his sister's defense. "Why would you want to take Flossie's prize away?" he demanded.

"What did you say your name was?" Mr. Bobbsey asked.

"I didn't," the man said angrily. "Now give me the house!"

All at once a voice came over the air-

port loudspeaker. "Will the Bobbsey family please meet Janis Wooley at the courtesy booth."

"Give it to me!" the man said loudly, grabbing for Flossie's prize, but Bert had placed himself in front of his sister, so the stranger could not get it.

Thinking quickly, Freddie raised his camera and took a picture. The flash going off startled the man.

"There's an airport guard," Nan said, pointing down the hall. "He'll straighten this out."

The man backed off, moving away. "Never mind," he snapped. "We'll . . . work this out later."

With that he walked quickly into the crowd and disappeared.

"What a mean man," Flossie said, hugging her house close to her.

"He certainly wanted your prize," Nan said. "I wonder why?"

"Well," Freddie said proudly, "I have

his picture." He pulled the dark photo out of the front of the instant developing camera. "In a minute we'll see how it turned out."

"Maybe we should meet Mrs. Wooley first, and do our detective work later," Mr. Bobbsey suggested.

Just then, the loudspeaker called their names again.

They quickly went to the courtesy booth. A woman with long auburn hair stood near it dressed in a brightly colored cotton skirt and sandals. She smiled at their approach.

"You must be the Bobbseys," she said. "I'm Janis Wooley. I'm representing the Oklahoma City Miniature Club. It will be my pleasure to be your hostess and guide during your stay in Oklahoma City."

"You seem a lot nicer than your friend," Freddie said, bobbing his curly blond head.

"My friend?" Janis Wooley asked.

"The man who met us at the gate," Nan explained.

"There's no one but me," the woman returned, looking puzzled. "And I wasn't on time, because someone pulled a prank on me and let all the air out of my left rear tire. Fortunately, I was able to make it to a gas station and get her only a little late."

Bert and Nan looked at each other. "Let her see the picture, Freddie," Bert said.

Freddie held out the fully developed snapshot. It clearly showed the tall man with the mean face trying to reach around Bert to grab Flossie's dollhouse.

"I've never seen this man before in my life!" Mrs. Wooley declared.

"This is getting more mysterious all the time," Nan said.

The Bobbseys took turns explaining what happened, leaving their hostess baffled. "It doesn't make any sense," she agreed.

"You have no idea either why someone would want Flossie's dollhouse?" Bert asked.

Mrs. Wooley shrugged. "We found the big dollhouse that Flossie so aptly named Gingerbread Manor—along with its miniature—in the basement of an old abandoned mansion, the Bacharach House. Gingerbread Manor is an exact duplicate of the Bacharach House and Flossie's miniature is an exact duplicate of both. The Bacharach House is being restored in preparation for Oklahoma's upcoming centennial celebration, and the Miniature Club is restoring the dollhouse. I don't know who that man is or why he'd be interested in Flossie's prize."

"Then I don't have to give it back?" Flossie asked.

Mrs. Wooley bent down in front of her, lifting the little girl's chin with an index finger. "Of course not," she said. "Gingerbread Manor is yours to keep for as long as you want it."

Then she straightened up, narrowing her eyes. "Although after today," she added, "you may not want to keep it."

Flossie stared at her, startled.

"Why not?" she asked, clutching her dollhouse closer to her.

A Shattered Screen

"I'll tell you later," Janis Wooley told Flossie. "Let's get going now." She led the Bobbseys through the airport terminal and down an escalator to the baggage claim area.

"While you're getting your suitcases, I'll drive the station wagon around to pick you up," she said. "Good thing we have one. A family like yours needs a big car."

Mr. Bobbsey chuckled. "I'll say," he commented. It was a fact he was very much aware of.

While they were waiting for their bags to come around on the revolving conveyor belt, Freddie studied the picture he had taken of the man who had tried to steal Flossie's house.

"How come he knew us?" Nan asked. "He spoke to us by name, as if he really had been sent to meet us."

"It was a clever lie," Bert said. "Let me see that house for a minute, Flossie."

Flossie hesitated. She seldom let the miniature Gingerbread Manor out of her reach. "Do you promise to be careful with it?" she asked her brother.

"Flossie!" Bert rolled his eyes to the ceiling.

"Oh, all right," the little girl replied, realizing he was getting irritated with her. She handed him the tiny toy.

Bert turned it around to look at all sides, but there was not much to see. Finally he gave it back, shrugging. "I wouldn't steal it," he said.

Soon, all the children were busy carrying their suitcases out to the waiting station wagon. Flossie and Freddie got to sit up front with Mrs. Wooley because Flossie was the guest of honor.

As they drove off, Freddie kept his camera up to his face the whole time so as not to miss the opportunity to snap a good picture.

But he didn't take many. He had bought the camera and film with his own saved-up money and couldn't afford to waste any shots.

It was a hot, dusty Oklahoma summer day, and Janis Wooley kept the air conditioner turned on high in the large, comfortable car. The land was flat and dotted everywhere with large pumping machines.

"What are those?" Freddie asked, lining one up in his viewfinder.

"Oil wells," Mrs. Wooley replied.

"They look like upside-down ice cream cones," Flossie said.

"Only while people are drilling," the woman answered. "Once the oil comes up, they put a pump on it."

Flossie looked at the pretty woman with the auburn hair. "Why did you say I might want to give up my dollhouse?"

"Well, I'll tell you," Mrs. Wooley said. "Part of your prize is that there's going to be a Flossie Bobbsey room in Gingerbread Manor! Since I'm an artist, as well as a lover of miniatures, I've been hired to do some sketches of you. Then, I'm going to make a lifelike Flossie Bobbsey doll to put in the room."

"Oh, no," Freddie said, turning his camera toward Flossie's chubby face. "One of her is enough!"

"With a Flossie Bobbsey doll in the Flossie Bobbsey room," Mrs. Wooley continued, "you might want to leave something in there for her to play with."

"That sounds nice, Flossie," Mrs. Bobbsey said from the back seat. "That way everyone can enjoy your lovely house."

Janis Wooley turned halfway in her seat. "I'm so happy all of you could come," she said.

Mr. Bobbsey spoke up. "After sending all that ebony wood out here for the Bacharach House restoration, I wanted to see what it had been used for."

He owned a lumberyard in the family's hometown of Lakeport, and had obtained the rare wood from an African supplier. It was at that time that Flossie found out about the contest.

"How is the project coming along?" her father went on.

Mrs. Wooley frowned as she turned from the highway onto a main thoroughfare. "Not well, I'm afraid. All the wood you sent has been stolen, and the restoration has been stopped."

"What!" Mr. Bobbsey exclaimed.

"How terrible," Nan cried.

"On top of that," Mrs. Wooley continued, "there have been reports of eerie noises coming from inside the house. When the police investigated, they found nothing."

"A haunted house!" Bert said, his face lighting up.

"Everyone's beginning to believe it," Janis Wooley replied.

"No," Flossie said, hugging the house close. "Gingerbread Manor is not haunted!"

"I hope you're right," the woman said. "The Bacharach House is one of the earliest mansions in Oklahoma. It would certainly make a fine addition to our centennial celebration."

"What's a scent-a-nail?" Flossie asked.

"Centennial," Nan replied from the back. "It means a hundred years."

Mrs. Wooley spoke up. "Oklahoma was opened up for settlement in 1889 by a huge land run. They lined up all the settlers in their wagons and fired a gun. The people raced across the territory and staked their claims—free land. Oklahoma City was founded on that day. The Bacharach House was built shortly thereafter."

She slowed down her car and turned in to a long drive that led to an immense, squat building. "This is the Omniplex," she said. "It's a museum where we keep the dollhouse. Would you like to see it before going to your hotel?"

"Yes! Yes!" Flossie squealed, and the others heartily agreed.

They parked the car and got out. The Omniplex shared a parking lot with another attraction that drew many people who were entering through large gates.

"What's that?" Bert wanted to know.

"The Oklahoma City Zoo," Mrs. Wooley said proudly. "One of the finest in the country."

"Can we go there?" Freddie asked

eagerly, pointing his camera in the direction of the zoo.

"Later," Mrs. Bobbsey laughed. "And you can take pictures of all the animals then."

They walked across the lot and into the building. Mrs. Wooley led them up the stairs to the second floor.

A large crowd had gathered there. Many people were pointing and yelling at a figure who was hurrying away in the other direction.

"The dollhouse!" Mrs. Wooley gasped. "Something must have happened."

She started running, and the Bobbseys followed close on her heels. They made their way through the crowd until they came to a security guard, who sat on the floor with his head in his hands. His hat lay beside him on the carpet. A huge, three-story dollhouse stood beside him, surrounded by a large plexiglass screen for protection.

The screen was shattered in several places, and slivers of plexiglass had fallen on the dollhouse. A heavy sledgehammer lay nearby.

"Oh, no!" Nan cried, as the others stared in disbelief. "Someone tried to destroy Gingerbread Manor!"

·3·

The Clue on the Hammer

Mr. Bobbsey knelt down next to the guard. "Are you all right?" he asked.

"I . . . I think so," the young man, who had a round face and sandy hair, said. He reached over and picked up his cap. The name *Jenkins* was written on a plate on his gray uniform. "A man pushed me against one of the support pillars and I fell."

Mr. Bobbsey checked Jenkins's head. He had a good-sized swelling just behind his left ear. An older man in a blue suit came along and squatted down next to Mr. Bobbsey.

"I'm Nathan Jacks, the museum director," he introduced himself.

"Jenkins got a bit of a bump here," Mr. Bobbsey said, pointing. "It would be advisable to get him to a doctor just to be sure he's okay."

"Good idea," Nathan Jacks agreed. "I'll bring my car around and take him myself." He patted the guard on the back. "You just take it easy until I come back for you, Jenkins."

"Yes, sir." The young man stood up on shaky legs, grinning sheepishly at the onlookers. "Show's over, folks," he told them, and they began to disperse.

Mrs. Wooley and the Bobbseys turned to the dollhouse to check for damage.

Flossie pressed her nose against the plexiglass and stared at the three-story, sixty-room mansion.

It was like something out of a storybook, much taller than she was, with high-peaked roofs, gingerbread trim, and tiny glittering lights in some of the rooms. The house was on rollers and its walls had been painted a lovely light blue with white trim. The interior was partially filled with miniature furniture from the 1890's. A tiny girl doll stood on a balcony, as though she were waiting for her friends to come for a party.

"It's bee-yoo-ti-ful," Flossie whispered, and pictured herself in such a fairytale.

"That man smashed up the barrier," Mrs. Wooley said, "but the house itself seems to be undamaged."

"Why would someone do such a terrible thing?" asked Nan, who stood beside Flossie, examining the house.

Mrs. Wooley shook her head. "I don't know. My husband is a detective on the Oklahoma City Police force. I'll see if he can help us get some answers. But then, you Bobbseys are pretty good detectives yourselves, aren't you?"

"That's right," Freddie said proudly. "I think we can solve this mystery!"

He had walked to the rail behind the

dollhouse. The second floor of the Omniplex was a mezzanine that overlooked the ground floor, which contained "hands on" science exhibits for children. The little boy stared at a rumbling earthquake model and a small hot air balloon that rose to the high ceiling from time to time. "May I go down there?" he asked eagerly.

"Go ahead, son," Mr. Bobbsey said from behind him. "We'll be here for a while."

"Thanks, Dad," Freddie said. "But first, I have some detective business to take care of."

Moving in front of Gingerbread Manor, he raised his camera and took a picture of the smashed barrier while Mrs. Wooley pulled large chunks of plexiglass off the dollhouse.

When the photo came out of the front of the camera, he handed it and his airport snapshot to Bert. "Take good care of the evidence," he told his brother, then hurried off to look at the science exhibits.

While Flossie helped Janis Wooley pull the debris from the dollhouse, Nan and Bert approached the young guard, who stood with his hand on the back of his neck.

"Do you feel well enough to answer a few questions?" Nan asked.

"Sure," Jenkins said. "They're probably making too much fuss over my head. I'm all right."

"What exactly happened?" Bert inquired.

"I was over by the Native American exhibits," the guard said, "when I saw this guy with gloves on carrying a sledgehammer. It looked really strange, too, because he was wearing a suit."

"Gloves, you say?" Nan asked.

Jenkins nodded.

"That means no fingerprints," Bert said. "What then?"

The guard bent his head back, rotating it slightly to loosen it up. "I watched him walk right up to the dollhouse. First he tried to rip out the barrier, and when it wouldn't budge, he started swinging the sledge. I yelled and ran over there; my shouts attracted a crowd real fast."

"The people probably scared him away," Nan said.

"Anyway," Jenkins continued, "I caught up to him and we scuffled, then I got knocked against the pole. A crowd started gathering, so he dropped the hammer and ran."

"Would you recognize him again if you saw him?"

"Sure," Jenkins answered.

"Would you take a look at this picture?" The boy handed the guard the snapshot Freddie had taken in the airport.

Jenkins looked at it, his eyes wide. "That's the one!" he shouted. "That's the man I fought with!"

Meanwhile, on the first floor of the museum, Freddie stood with his face glued to the viewer of an old periscope. It had been taken from a World War II submarine. The periscope went from the first floor all the way up through the top of the building and offered a good view of the roads and houses that surrounded the Omniplex.

"Freddie!"

The little boy looked up to see his father waving for him to join them again. Reluctantly he left the periscope.

When he reached the others on the second floor, everyone was excitedly talking about the fact that the man who had approached them in the airport was the same one who had tried to destroy the dollhouse.

"What is it about these twin houses?" Nan asked, puzzled.

"They're really triplets," Flossie said. She was still staring at Gingerbread Manor and didn't even turn around. "The real house is just like these two, remember?"

"And we're having trouble there, too," Mrs. Wooley added sadly.

Freddie looked at the vandal's sledge-hammer, which lay by the pole Jenkins had fallen against. Thinking it might be a good idea to get a picture of the tool, he picked it up to lean it against the pole. That's when he saw the inscription.

"Oh no," he exclaimed. Everyone looked at him.

"What is it?" Nan asked. "What's wrong?"

"Look for yourself," Freddie said, and carried the weighty hammer over to the others.

They gathered around and stared in amazement. There, inlaid in the polished handle, was the inscription: *Bobbsey Lumberyard.*

·4·

Monkeyshines

"That man must have stolen the hammer from my place in Lakeport!" Mr. Bobbsey fumed.

"But why would he do that?" Nan said, puzzled. "He could have used something else to shatter the plexiglass."

"Maybe he wanted to incriminate us," Bert said darkly.

"Well, if that was his plan, it didn't work!" Mrs. Wooley declared. "Now, let me take you to your hotel. And then we'd better report everything to the police."

A few minutes later, she was driving them through the heavy city traffic.

"There's the Oklahoma capitol building," she said, pointing through the windshield at a huge square structure with tall pillars and hundreds of steps leading up to the entrance. "That's where they make the laws. Your hotel is just down the street."

She guided the station wagon along Lincoln Boulevard, past dozens of hotels and motels on either side.

"I thought capitol buildings had big domes on the top," Bert said, turning to take another look through the back window.

Mrs. Wooley smiled. "I don't know about all of them," she said, "but this one was supposed to have a dome. They just never got around to making it."

Everyone laughed.

A moment later, their hostess pulled into the parking lot of the hotel and drove up to the big front doors so that the porter could take the Bobbseys' luggage up to their rooms.

"Why don't you get settled in and have

lunch?" she suggested as they piled out.
"I'll call my husband and tell him about
what happened at the Omniplex and the
airport. That way you won't have to go to
the police station. Then, in about an
hour, I want to do some sketches of Flossie for the doll."

"Oh goody!" Flossie said, excited at
the prospect of being an artist's model.

"That doesn't sound like much fun to
me," Freddie objected.

"I have an idea," Mr. Bobbsey said. "If
Mrs. Wooley would lend us her car while
she sketches, the rest of us could visit the
zoo."

"Great!" Freddie said, perking up. Nan
and Bert excitedly agreed.

The children checked into two rooms:
boys in one, girls in the other. A message
had been waiting for Mr. Bobbsey at the
desk. It said to contact Dinah, their
housekeeper, in Lakeport.

Everyone gathered around the phone
in his room when he was ready to make

the call. "I hope there's no trouble at home," he said, worried.

He dialed the number and waited. Dinah Johnson answered after several rings.

"Mr. Bobbsey," she said. "I'm sorry to bother you, but I thought I should tell you something."

"What is it?" Mr. Bobbsey asked.

"A man called," she replied. "He wanted to know when your plane would land in Oklahoma City."

"Did he give his name?"

"No. He just said he was from the Miniature Club, so I told him. But afterward, I realized they knew when you were scheduled to land, so I got worried."

Mr. Bobbsey thanked her, then hung up and told the others what Dinah had said.

"I'll bet it was that man who met us," Bert declared.

"That's how he knew we'd be there,"

Nan said. "But how did he find out about us in the first place?"

"Maybe he read about us in the newspaper," Freddie suggested, "or watched us on TV."

"But why is he after us?" Flossie asked.

"He's not after us," Nan said. "He's after the two dollhouses for some reason." She picked up the miniature from its resting place on the bed and looked at it. "But what could that reason be?"

"Maybe," Mr. Bobbsey said, "a nice lunch would help us think better."

Everyone agreed and they went to the hotel coffee shop.

After a pleasant meal, they met Mrs. Wooley, who was waiting for them, car keys in hand, in the lobby.

"If it's all right with you," she said, "Flossie and I will work in her room while you go to the zoo. Can you find your way back there?"

"Sure," Mr. Bobbsey said.

They hopped into the car and drove off, but he had to ask for directions four times before they finally made it.

Mrs. Wooley had Flossie sit in the light coming through the window while she sketched the girl's face on a large drawing pad. She held the pencil lightly in the palm of her hand, bracing it with her thumb. Her strokes were thick and bold.

"You certainly fidget a lot," she smiled at the chubby blond child.

Flossy giggled. "Daddy says I have ants in my pants, but I checked them before and didn't find anything."

"Well, we won't work too long," the woman said with a smile.

Flossie liked that idea. As much as she enjoyed the attention, she couldn't help wondering what she was missing at the zoo. "Did you talk to your husband about the man at the airport?" she asked finally.

"Yes," Mrs. Wooley answered, brushing her long hair from her face. "He's as

mystified as we are and can't think of any reason why these things are happening."

"I can't figure out how he got Daddy's sled hammer," Flossie said.

Janis laughed. "That's sledgehammer, Flossie, and I'm just as puzzled as you. But there must be a reason," she said. "I wouldn't be surprised if the same man let the air out of my tires so I couldn't pick you up on time."

Meanwhile, the rest of the Bobbseys walked along a beautiful tree-lined path in the zoo. Most of the animals were housed in exhibits that were like their native habitats. There were very few cages and so there were many happy residents from all over the world.

Eventually, the family split up. Freddie went to the petting zoo, while Mr. and Mrs. Bobbsey fed the ducks in the big pond by the picnic area. Bert and Nan took the opportunity to revisit some of their favorite exhibits.

While they were walking around, they passed a gray-suited attendant throwing fish to the sea lions in the aquarena. Suddenly Nan froze, her hand on Bert's arm to slow him down.

"What's the matter?" he asked.

"Look over there," Nancy whispered, "at the man feeding the sea lions."

Bert turned, and his eyes widened. "It's that guy again," he said. "The man from the airport. He must work here. Quick, you go tell Mom and Dad, while I keep an eye on him."

Nan hurried off. She found her parents at the duck pond and told them the story. Mr. Bobbsey decided to call the police, while Mrs. Bobbsey went looking for Freddie. When Nan returned to the aquarena, Bert and the mystery man were gone. Frantically, she searched the immediate area, finally ending up in a long, low building with the word *Simians* painted on the outside.

Bert stood in a corner watching the suspect, who was casually dressed in a western shirt and khakis. He was in a cage, bringing bananas to a pair of large gorillas. Their screeching sounds echoed through the building.

"Has he seen you?" Nan whispered to her brother.

The boy shook his head. "I don't think so."

"I'm going out to wait for Dad," Nan said.

She left the dark building and squinted into the bright sunshine. Almost immediately, she saw Mr. Bobbsey, a man in a blue suit, and several uniformed policemen coming toward her.

"Over here!" she called, pointing to the simian building. "He's in there. So is Bert."

Cautiously they entered. Bert was gesturing to the cage holding the suspect. The man in the suit nodded and walked up to him flanked by a policeman on either side.

"Police," he said, flipping open his wallet to reveal a badge for the suspect to see. "I'd like to ask you a few questions."

The man stared at him angrily, then threw the bananas on the floor. "You want to talk to me?" he challenged. "Then come in and get me!"

With that, he walked to the door and slammed it shut, locking himself in the cage with the huge gorillas!

·5·

A Rare Bird

The man stood in the gorilla cage with his arms folded in front, while the large black apes moved slowly around him. They looked him up and down, grunting and poking him from time to time.

"Come on out of there," the detective ordered. "You may get hurt!"

"Leave me alone," the man said. "Go away."

"We're not going anywhere," one of the uniformed officers spoke up. "So you may as well come out."

"No!"

The detective walked over to Mr. Bobbsey. "Are you connected with the zoo?" he asked.

"Why no," Mr. Bobbsey replied. "We were visiting here when we saw this man, who had vandalized the dollhouse exhibit at the Omniplex."

The detective looked puzzled. "You mean, this isn't about the zoo thefts?"

"Zoo thefts?" Bert and Nan said at the same time.

The detective looked at them. "Perhaps you'd better explain," he said.

Bert and Nan began the story, Freddie and Mrs. Bobbsey joining the group as they talked. When they were finished, the policeman smiled.

"Well, first of all," he said, "let me introduce myself. I'm John Wooley."

"Mrs. Wooley's husband!" Freddie exclaimed.

"Right. Janis has already filled me in on the case. Secondly, I'd like to tell you that the exploits of the famous Bobbsey

detectives are well known, even in Oklahoma City. I'm glad to meet all of you."

Freddie walked up to the gorilla cage and took a picture of the man inside.

"What's this about zoo thefts?" Bert asked.

Nan pointed to the man in the cage, who was now being shoved around by the apes. "If that man works here," she said, "maybe he's involved in both cases."

"I didn't do anything!" the suspect shouted.

"Then come out!" Detective Wooley demanded. He looked at the children. "Are you sure this guy is your man?"

"Yes," Freddie said. "I took his picture at the airport." He rummaged in his pocket. "See?"

"That's good enough for me," John Wooley said, after inspecting the photograph.

Just then, a pudgy little man in a wrinkled suit came running into the building and hurried up to the group.

"What is it? What's happening?"

"Mr. Fiala," John Wooley said, "I'd like you to meet the Bobbsey family—"

"Minus one," Nan said.

The detective continued. "This is Mr. Fiala, the zoo director."

"Have you caught the animal thief?" Mr. Fiala asked.

"No, sir," Detective Wooley said, and told the story. Mr. Fiala became concerned and walked over to the cage.

"Come on out, Denny," he said. "It's dangerous to stay in there too long."

"Tell them to go away," the man returned.

"I can't do that," Mr. Fiala said. "But I can talk to them for you, if you'd like."

"Promise?"

"I promise."

The man hesitated for just a moment before making his way to the cage door.

He opened it and hurried out, the uniformed officers immediately grabbing him.

Mr. Fiala wiped his wire-rimmed glasses on a handkerchief. "I'm afraid you people have the wrong man," he said. "That man's Denny Cole. And he couldn't have done any of the things you said because he's been here with me all day."

"No," Bert said. "That can't be. We saw him at the airport this morning."

Freddie handed Mr. Fiala the photo. "See? We even took his picture."

The director stared at the snapshot. "It certainly looks like Denny," he admitted. "But I know Denny's been here all day because he's been helping me clean out an old storeroom."

"Why did he lock himself in the cage, then?" Nan asked. "That's not how an innocent man would act."

They all turned to Denny Cole.

"When I was a kid," he said, "I got into trouble and was sent to reform school. Guess I've been scared of the police ever since."

"You're sure he wasn't out of your sight this morning?" Detective Wooley asked Mr. Fiala.

"Positive," the zoo director replied.

The detective shrugged apologetically at the Bobbseys. "Guess it was a wild goose chase."

"We're really sorry," Nan told Denny Cole.

The man nodded. "It could have happened to anybody. I'm not mad at you."

"Go on back to work, Denny," Mr. Fiala said.

"Yes, sir," the man answered, hurrying off.

"We'd like to apologize to you, too," Bert told the zoo director. "We really thought we had the right guy."

"No harm done. Except," said Mr.

Fiala, turning to the gorilla cage, "you've given the gorillas something to talk about for a few days."

Everyone laughed in relief.

"What about the thefts?" Freddie asked, taking back his photograph.

Mr. Fiala frowned. "Now, there's a problem," he admitted. "Over the last three months, several rare and valuable animals have disappeared from the zoo. Just recently, we lost a snow leopard and a panda on the same day."

"Why would someone steal animals?" Bert asked.

"Money," Mr. Fiala answered. "There are many unscrupulous collectors out there who would pay dearly for an animal of a rare or endangered species. Why, right now we have an ivory-billed wood-pecker on loan from the San Diego Zoo that would bring upwards of fifty thousand dollars on the black market."

Nan whistled. "That's a lot of money," she said.

"Any leads?" Bert asked.

"Not a one," the man replied deject-
edly.

Flossie had to rest for a minute at the
top of the long flight of steps leading up
to the Oklahoma capitol. "There must be
thirty hundred steps," she said.

"Not quite that many," Mrs. Wooley
replied. "But it is a tiring walk. Coming
up here was a good idea, though, you'll
see."

Flossie nodded. "I thought it would be
fun to sightsee when you got finished
drawing, since the rest of the family's
doing it too."

"Ready to go in?" Mrs. Wooley asked.

Flossie nodded, hoping that walking
back down would be easier than the trip
up had been.

They moved into the building to the
sound of trumpets and drums. The ro-
tunda was full of people and music, because it was high school band day at the

capitol. Just then, the band from Putnam City High played "Oklahoma" and the audience clapped along. Mrs. Wooley and Flossie walked through the crowd, admiring the state seal inlaid in the floor and the giant paintings on the wall. But Flossie felt uneasy, as if someone were watching her. She kept looking over her shoulder, clutching her miniature dollhouse close to her.

The band finished and another took its place. In the milling crowd, Flossie and Mrs. Wooley were momentarily separated.

The little girl felt uneasy again, and all at once a curious sensation overtook her.

She turned quickly, and there he was—the man from the airport!

"No!" Flossie screamed, but the cry was lost in the music of the Northwest Classen band.

Anger lined the man's face as he took a step and reached for her!

·6·

Spooky Mansion

The stranger grabbed Flossie by the arm so she couldn't run.

"No!" she screamed. "Help!"

But no one heard her. "Shut up!" the man said sharply. "Give me that house!" He snatched it from her, pushing her to the ground.

"Stop that!" a woman yelled.

Flossie looked up through a forest of knees to see Mrs. Wooley running to her just as the man disappeared into the crowd.

"Are you all right?" Janis Wooley asked as she bent to help Flossie up.

"That man took Gingerbread Manor," the little girl cried. "He was the one we saw at the airport. We have to catch him!"

Nan, Bert and Freddie sat on the bed in the girls' hotel room, looking at the sketches Janis Wooley had made of Flossie.

"She's a really good artist," Nan said, as she studied a page containing several angles of her sister's face. "These look just like Flossie."

"Yes." Freddie grinned impishly. "Mrs. Wooley even got Flossie's big mouth just right."

"Freddie . . ." Bert scolded.

Just then, the door opened and Flossie and Janis Wooley walked in. The woman had her arm around Flossie's shoulder and it was obvious that the little girl had been crying.

"What happened?" Bert said, hurrying over to them.

"That man from the airport got my house," Flossie said. "He pushed me down and took it away from me."

Hearing the commotion, Mr. and Mrs. Bobbsey appeared through the door.

"The same man?" Mr. Bobbsey asked.

Mrs. Wooley nodded. "I saw him too," she said.

"That proves we were wrong about the zoo," Bert said.

"The zoo?" Flossie asked.

Freddie showed Flossie the picture of the man in the cage. "We found him at the zoo," he said. "When we called the police, Mr. Wooley showed up, and it turned out we had the wrong man. He just looked like our suspect."

"You met John?" Mrs. Wooley beamed.

"He was very nice, too," Nan added, "considering we called him out for nothing."

"But why would that thief go to so much trouble for Flossie's dollhouse?" Freddie asked.

"And the bigger one at the Mommy-plex," Flossie added.

"That's Omniplex," Nan corrected. Then she turned to her father. "Dad, can I ask you a question?"

"Sure, sweetheart."

"Did you ship the ebony wood to Oklahoma yourself, or did you have the African supplier send it directly?"

"I shipped it. It was part of a large import order I contracted for."

"Was the wood all you sent?" Bert asked.

Mr. Bobbsey looked puzzled for a moment, then he snapped his fingers. "No," he said excitedly. "A number of tools went out also. I'd forgotten about that because it was handled by my foreman."

"That's it!" Nan said. "Whoever stole the wood from the Bacharach mansion took the sledgehammer from there, too."

"And then he tried to wreck Gingerbread Manor," Freddie added, while lining up a camera shot of Mrs. Wooley's sketches.

"And stole my miniature dollhouse," Flossie put in.

"I'm sorry, dear," Mrs. Bobbsey added sympathetically.

There was silence in the room for a moment. Finally Nan said, "There must be something—some . . . secret that all the houses share. Maybe it's time to go out to the Bacharach mansion and look it over."

"Can we, Dad?" Freddie asked.

"It's fine with me," Mr. Bobbsey replied. "I'd like to see for myself what my wood will be used for."

Janis Wooley smiled. "I know what a detective on a case is like," she joked. "Why don't you take the car and follow my directions to Heritage Hills. I'll stay here and see if I can talk Mrs. Bobbsey into doing some shopping."

Mary Bobbsey brightened. "That sounds wonderful."

A few minutes later, Mr. Bobbsey and the twins were on their way to Heritage Hills, the oldest residential section in Oklahoma City. It was a historical preservation area, where all the houses were kept up just as they had been in the early 1900's. The Bacharach mansion was located right in the middle of the Hills district. The children recognized it immediately. It looked just like the miniatures!

A large expanse of tree-lined lawn separated the huge house from the street. Mr. Bobbsey headed down the long, circular gravel drive to the front entrance. Scraps of wood were scattered on the grass, and a man was walking among the debris, taking notes on a yellow pad.

He came over to the car when they pulled up. "Can I help you?" he asked suspiciously, and leaned down to the driver's window.

Mr. Bobbsey stuck his head out. "My name's Bobbsey," he said.

"Richard Bobbsey?" the man asked.

"Yes," Mr. Bobbsey anwered, surprised.

The man shook his hand. "My name's Jack Howard. We've spoken over the phone."

"Oh, yes. You're the contractor doing the restoration," Mr. Bobbsey said. "Glad to meet you. What's going on out here?"

The man pointed his thumb toward the lawn. "You're looking at all that's left of your shipment. Someone stole all the wood, and we had to stop work on the house."

"Were any tools stolen?" Nan asked from beside her father.

"Sure enough," Jack Howard replied. "They went along with the wood. Strangest thing I ever saw."

"What do you mean?" Bert asked as the Bobbseys climbed out of the station wagon.

"It would take several trucks to haul away that much stuff," the man returned. "But no one in the neighborhood saw or heard anything. And then there are those noises that come from inside the house. They have scared my men half to death. Everyone thinks the place is haunted. I couldn't get my people out here to work on a bet right now."

"*Is* the house haunted?" Flossie asked.

The man raised his eyebrows. "You tell me," he said.

"Are you going to replace the materials?" Mr. Bobbsey asked.

"I suppose so," Jack Howard replied.

"Maybe we can go over your requirements now."

The man nodded, holding up his pad. "I've been making a list."

"Can we go in the house?" Freddie asked.

"If it's all right with your father," Jack Howard said, "it's just fine with me."

Mr. Bobbsey nodded. "Be careful

though," he warned. "There's probably a lot of junk lying around."

"And no electricity," Mr. Howard added.

The twins nodded in unison and cautiously walked up the stairs to the wide porch. The house was dark and dreary. In poor repair, it looked sinister, not at all the bright, cheery Gingerbread Manor of Flossie's fantasy.

The front door creaked loudly when they pushed it open. It was dark inside, the late afternoon sun having slipped behind the neighboring houses.

"This is creepy," Flossie said, making sure she was close enough to Nan to reach out and touch her.

"Awww, no it's not," Freddie countered, but when he raised his camera to his face to take a picture of what he could not even see, his hands were shaking badly.

The flash of the camera was bright, making everyone jump with fright. When

they realized what it was, they all laughed with relief.

"No more of that," Bert told Freddie. "You should have warned us."

"Sorry," Freddie said, embarrassed to say he was just as frightened as the rest of them.

Suddenly a low moan echoed through the old house. The twins stopped moving, staring all around.

Now a cry seemed to come from nowhere and everywhere at the same time, oozing from the walls and ceiling. It was a disembodied, ghostly voice!

The Wrong Suspect

The wail grew louder, screeching through the house. It sounded almost like a baby crying, but not quite.

"Oooo-eeee," Flossie whined, hugging herself closer to Nan.

"Where's it coming from?" Bert asked, staring into the darkness.

"I . . . I can't tell," Nan replied, happy to have Flossie to hold on to.

All at once, the front door opened wide! The twins jumped, yelling, only to be confronted by Mr. Bobbsey and Jack Howard.

"See what I mean?" Mr. Howard said, frowning at the ghostly racket. "Is it any wonder I can't keep help out here?"

"Let's look for the source of the sound," Mr. Bobbsey decided rather bravely. "It has to be coming from somewhere."

"We'll have to hurry," Bert said. "It's getting darker in here by the minute."

"Let's break into teams," Nan suggested, "and search different sections of the house."

"Good idea," Mr. Bobbsey agreed.

"I have some flashlights in my pickup," Jack Howard said, and hurried out to get them.

When he returned, the group divided. Mr. Howard, Bert, and Freddie were on one team; Mr. Bobbsey, Nan, and Flossie on the other. Each team got a large flashlight to show them the way in the quickly-diminishing light.

They searched as fast and as much as they could. Flossie didn't realize just how many rooms sixty were until she had to go through half of them one by one. The house was dilapidated, but still beautiful, and the twin recognized many of the rooms from her own tiny mansion.

She wondered if the dollhouse had been built for a child to play with, a little girl who lived a long time ago, and who might be someone's great-grandmother now. The Bacharach family had left Oklahoma fifty years before, never to return. Their lives were a mystery, just like their house.

The moaning continued periodically during the search, but the Bobbseys found nothing. Finally, they gave up and went out.

They stood on the front lawn, watching the mansion fade, as twilight turned the Oklahoma sky a brilliant purple.

"Maybe we're not meant to restore this beautiful old place," Jack Howard said, scratching his nearly bald head.

"Yes you are," Flossie said with conviction.

"There have to be answers to this mystery," Nan said.

"And we're going to find them," Freddie added, as he studied the out-of-focus picture he had taken inside the house. It was nothing but a blurry wall.

The family returned to the hotel. Darkness had settled in by the time they arrived. It was late, almost past the younger twins' bedtime. And they had all been so busy, they hadn't even had dinner!

Mrs. Bobbsey was waiting for them, and they headed for the hotel restaurant.

After a fine main course of Oklahoma chicken-fried steak and mashed potatoes, everyone had pecan pie and milk.

"This was really good," Flossie said as she toyed with the last bits of pie crust, "but I sure miss Dinah's home cooking."

"I miss Waggo," Freddie said, thinking of their family dog. "I wonder what Waggo, Sam, and Dinah are doing right now?"

"Probably enjoying some peace and

quiet," Mr. Bobbsey joked.

After paying the check, the family strolled leisurely through the lobby, the children lagging behind their parents.

"Look!" Nan said suddenly, and pointed. "Over there!"

By the front door, casually reading a newspaper, was Denny Cole, the man from the gorilla cage. He was still wearing the same khaki pants and western-style shirt he had worn at the zoo earlier.

"Him again!" Freddie cried out.

"It's the man who took my house!" Flossie said angrily.

Without a thought, she marched over to where the man stood. The others followed reluctantly.

"Give me my dollhouse back," the little girl demanded.

"Leave me alone, kid," the suspect replied. "I don't even know who you are, and I sure don't have your dollhouse."

"You took it!" Flossie accused him, standing her ground. "Now give it back!"

"Beat it!" the man snapped, then looked up and saw the other twins. "You again. Why don't you leave me alone?"

Nan gently pulled her sister away from Denny Cole. "That's not the man who took your house," she said. "He just looks like him. His name's Denny Cole, and he works at the zoo."

"I don't care!" Flossie returned. "I want my dollhouse."

Nan apologized to Denny Cole and took Flossie upstairs to their room.

The girls shared a large bed and soon they fell fast asleep.

Nan awoke the next morning and noticed that the rest of the family had come into their room and were gathered around the television set. Bert was pointing to the picture.

"There's Mr. Fiala," he said.

Puzzled, Nan rubbed her eyes, woke Flossie, and slid down to the end of the bed. Sure enough, there on the screen was the zoo director. Detective Wooley was in the background giving orders to uniformed policemen.

". . . happened last night not long after dark," Mr. Fiala was saying. "Someone sneaked in and got away with an ivory-billed woodpecker on loan from the San Diego Zoo."

"What was the bird worth?" a reporter asked him, as a picture of the sleek, long-billed bird with a fiery tuft on its head came onto the screen.

"It's a rare and valuable bird," Mr. Fiala said sadly. "It's worth a great deal of money, but its value is far greater than money could ever buy. As a nearly extinct species, it represents one of the last of its kind. Its beauty may never be seen on the earth again!"

"I can't believe it," Nan said, a tear coming to her eye. "Someone stole that beautiful bird!"

"It was the man who stole my doll-house, Denny Cole," Flossie insisted.

·8·

The Secret Room

"Have you forgotten that we were with Mr. Cole when your dollhouse was taken?" Bert reminded his sister. "And as far as the zoo theft goes, Denny was right here in this hotel arguing with you when the zoo was broken into."

"I don't know *how* he did it," Flossie said. "I only know that he did."

The phone on the nightstand rang loudly, stopping the discussion. Mr. Bobbsey answered.

"Hello, Mrs. Wooley," he said into the receiver. "We've just been watching your husband on TV. Yes, it's a terrible thing. Certainly. We'll see you in the lobby."

Mr. Bobbsey hung up the phone and clapped his hands. "Okay, everybody. Let's hurry and get dressed. We're going to meet Mrs. Wooley for breakfast."

The Bobbseys met their hostess and had pancakes in the coffee shop. Janis Wooley had eaten with her husband, so she only drank some juice.

"Are there any leads on the zoo case?" Bert asked her as he finished off the last bite.

The woman sadly shook her head. "The theft was just like the others," she said. "Someone who apparently knew what he was doing took a valuable animal, and got away clean."

"Maybe it was an inside job," Bert said.

"That's certainly a possibility," Mrs. Wooley replied, "but the zoo employees always seem to have alibis."

"Even Denny Cole?" Flossie asked.

"You should know," Janis Wooley

smiled. "*You* provided his alibi last night."

"I didn't want to," Flossie returned, and poured some more syrup on her pancakes.

"What's on the agenda for today?" Mrs. Bobbsey asked.

"Well," Janis replied, "today they'll finish up work on Gingerbread Manor for the presentation tomorrow. There are, as always, many fine exhibits at the Omniplex. Also, a sightseeing bus tour of Oklahoma City leaves from the zoo in about thirty minutes."

"I'd like to take that," Mrs. Bobbsey said to her husband.

He patted her hand. "That sounds good to me. I'll go with you."

Bert and Nan decided to explore the exhibits in greater detail, while Flossie and Freddie wanted to watch the finishing touches being put on Gingerbread Manor. They would meet their parents at the Omniplex later.

The group drove in the already hot morning air to the large complex, where Mr. and Mrs. Bobbsey got off at the bus stop.

Once in the Omniplex, Bert and Nan made their way through the fine Native American handcrafts and artwork displays, enjoying the treasures of a culture alive just a few hundred years ago, yet almost prehistoric in its nature.

Freddie and Flossie accompanied Mrs. Wooley to the dollhouse, surprised to find her husband among the many workers fussing with the structure.

"What are you doing here?" Janis asked him.

John Wooley shrugged. "I'm checking every lead I can find," he said. "Yesterday, the Bobbseys seemed to be connecting the zoo thefts with the vandalism here."

"The same man did both things," Flossie chimed in.

"Let me see your pictures again, Freddie," the detective requested, and studied the snapshots intensely. "They sure look alike," he said. "It could be the same man."

"Are you sure the zoo director's telling the truth?" Flossie asked.

Mrs. Wooley nodded. "Mr. Fiala is above suspicion. He's a fine man."

"I wish you'd get this settled," Mrs. Wooley said to her husband with a smile. "I'd like to see you home for dinner once in a while."

The detective sighed as he looked at the extra security personnel by the dollhouse. "If I don't solve the zoo case, my boss will fire me!" he said. "So I'd better be going."

The Bobbseys waved and watched him wander away. When he was gone, Flossie turned to the dollhouse.

It was almost ready now. People were working quickly at the open sections, filling rooms with ornate furniture from the era of Queen Victoria, or hanging up tiny strips of small-scale wallpaper. There were miniature baby grand pianos and doll-sized crystal chandeliers, complete with real wax candles no bigger than toothpicks.

Mrs. Wooley came up next to Flossie and put an arm on her shoulder. "This is the Flossie Bobbsey Room," she said, pointing to a still unfurnished bedroom on the third floor. "It's where the doll that looks like you will live."

"She'll be unhappy," Flossie said.

"Why?" Janis Wooley asked.

"Because she won't have a pretty miniature dollhouse to play with!"

Mrs. Wooley hugged her. "I'm so sorry, honey," she said.

Flossie smiled sadly. "It's a nice dollhouse anyway," she said. "But I'm surprised at the Flossie Bobbsey Room."

"Surprised?" Mrs. Wooley replied.

"Instead of a bedroom, I thought you'd

use the secret playroom," Flossie said.

Everyone stopped working and turned to Flossie.

"Secret playroom?" a tall skinny woman asked.

"Sure," Flossie said. "Over here."

The little girl moved around the house to the steps leading up to the back porch. She bent to examine the stairs, then pulled out one of the sections.

It hinged open with a jerk, revealing a door that was hidden by the stairs.

"See?" Flossie said.

Everyone excitedly crowded around her as she opened the tiny door onto a small indoor stairway that led into a secret room next to the basement.

"That little girl had to come all the way across the country to show us how our dollhouse works!" a young woman with long black hair exclaimed.

"I hope we don't have to furnish the new room," someone else said and everyone laughed.

Freddie stepped up to the secret room and took a picture. He knew a clue when he saw one!

"I wonder," Flossie whispered to him when he was finished, "if the real Bacharach mansion has a secret room, too?"

Freddie stared at his sister. "Maybe it does!

·9·

A Dangerous Cat

After hearing the shouts coming from the vicinity of Gingerbread Manor, Nan and Bert abandoned their museum tour and hurried over to the dollhouse.

"That may be it!" Nan said when she saw the secret room behind the back steps. "It may be the clue we've been looking for!"

"You really think so?" Mrs. Wooley asked.

"Sure," Bert agreed. "The secret room may be the link between all the houses.

We have to get over to the Bacharach mansion right away!"

"What about your parents?" Mrs. Wooley asked.

"We'll leave a message for them," Bert said. "They can join us there." He asked one of the workers to look out for his mother and father and tell them what happened.

Then, without wasting another minute, they all hurried out to Mrs. Wooley's car and drove to Heritage Hills. The strong Oklahoma wind made the overgrown mimosa trees dance eerily on the long gravel drive leading to the mansion, which seemed to be deserted.

"Sure is spooky," Flossie said.

"Don't be scared," Freddie told her. "I'm here to protect you."

He picked up his collection of pictures and sorted through them. Suddenly he stopped, frowning at the out-of-focus photo he had taken inside the house.

Something was in it that he hadn't noticed before!

"What's this?" he asked, pointing to a blurry, grill-like section of wall near the floor.

Janis Wooley parked the car and looked closely at the photo. "It's a crude form of central heating," she said. "These old houses were built before people had furnaces, but many of them were outfitted with central heat when it was invented. The conduits are very large and connect in the basement somewhere."

"They go all through the house?" Nan asked.

"I believe so."

"So a loud noise coming from the basement area could easily travel through the whole house by way of these large vents?" Bert inquired.

"You mean the ghost noises!" Flossie said, her eyes brightening.

Her brother nodded, and Nan spoke

up. "But we checked the basement yesterday when we were looking for the source of the sounds. There was no furnace anywhere."

"The secret room!" Flossie exclaimed. "It must be in the secret room!"

They were eager as well as a little frightened when they climbed out of the station wagon. But the excitement was much greater than the fear, and they all hurried to the back steps without another thought.

"Look here," Bert said, pointing to the ground near the rickety back steps.

The tall grass was flattened out in a semicircle from the stairs.

"The steps *do* swing open!" Nan exclaimed. "And somebody's been down there recently."

Bert and Freddie were already tugging on the wooden stairs. The section swung open easily, revealing a secret door behind!

"Maybe we shouldn't go down," Mrs. Wooley cautioned. "We have no idea what we'll find."

"But it may answer a lot of important questions," Nan urged.

The dark-haired girl moved to the door and turned the handle cautiously. It opened easily to a flight of cement steps that ended in total darkness.

"We should have brought flashlights," Freddie said.

"Wait," Flossie called. "There are candles."

A cardboard box filled with long candles sat on the top step. Everyone took one, and Mrs. Wooley lighted them.

The young detectives marched down the stairs like a procession, each one sinking slowly into the darkness. The air smelled musty, but the passage was remarkably clean and free from dust and spider webs.

Once they all gathered at the bottom, their combined candles threw off enough

light to illuminate the secret room. It was filled with long planks of finely-honed black wood!

"Ebony," Bert exclaimed, bending to examine it. "It couldn't be anything else."

"And look here!" Flossie said excitedly. "Tools!"

They went over and stared at two crates full of tools, which had *Bobbsey Lumberyard* printed on them.

"It's Dad's stuff all right," Bert said. "The thief hid it down here."

"That's why nobody in the neighborhood saw the wood being hauled away," Nan reasoned. "It never left the place!"

"Well, I think we've seen enough," Mrs. Wooley said. "Let's get out of here and call my husband."

"There's a door in the far wall," Freddie said, pointing. "Maybe it leads to another secret room!"

"We'll let John check it out," Janis insisted. "Let's go now."

Reluctantly, the Bobbseys climbed back up the stairs.

"We'll have to find a pay phone," Mrs. Wooley said, once they were outside again.

"Why not leave us here to stand guard?" Freddie suggested. "We'll hide in the bushes, and if anyone shows up, we can report it to you when you come back."

The woman thought for a moment. "Well, I don't need you to make a phone call," she admitted at last. "But you must promise to stay out of trouble."

"We will!" the twins said in unison, four heads bobbing up and down.

As soon as Janis Wooley had left, Freddie said, "I think we should go down and check that other room."

"But you said we'd stay up here," Flossie said.

Freddie shook his head. "No. I said we'd stay out of trouble."

"It doesn't matter anyway," Bert declared. "How would we light the candles to go back down?"

Freddie smiled. "I never put mine out," he said, pulling the lit candle from behind his back.

The others laughed, then relit their candles on Freddie's and eagerly returned to the secret room. The first thing Freddie did was take a picture of the woodpile.

"It's my chain of evidence," he said proudly.

Bert moved toward the connecting door. "Ready?" he asked, his hand on the knob.

The others nodded, and he swung the door open. Everyone gasped.

The room was like a treasure chest, filled with antiques of every kind— ornate oil lamps, paintings, and beautiful hand-carved furniture.

"What a collection!" Nan exclaimed. "Some of this must be more than a hundred years old."

"And there's so much of it!" Flossie

said in awe. "Whoever lived here must have left in a hurry to forget so many wonderful things."

"Come over here!" Freddie called, and hurried to a corner of the dark, shadowy room.

The others followed him to a huge, rusted metal box that was connected to the ceiling by a large pipe.

"The central heating unit," Nan exclaimed. "So the noise could have come from here, couldn't it?"

As if in answer to her remark, they heard loud hammering.

"What's that?" Flossie asked, frightened.

The sound stopped abruptly, only to start again seconds later. It continued for several moments, then ceased again.

"Let's follow the noise," Nan suggested, walking farther into the dark room.

They moved cautiously, as the noise was getting louder. Then they found the source.

"A bird," Flossie cried, pointing to a

cage suspended on a wooden support pil-
lar.

"Not just any bird," Nan said, holding
her light higher to shine more fully on
the animal. "It's an ivory-billed wood-
pecker!"

The bird cocked its head to look at
them, then returned to pecking for bugs
on the wooden post.

"The zoo thieves must have hidden it
here!" Freddie exclaimed.

"Here's more," Bert said, moving toward the back wall.

There, on the floor, sat a huge panda,
its black-masked eyes staring sadly
at the children. It was tied to the wall
with a short chain and looked helpless
and pitiful.

"Here's another chain," Nan said, indi-
cating a spot a distance from the panda.
"But it's been broken."

"What could have been—" Bert began,
but was interrupted by a loud growl from
behind.

They all whirled around. There, between them and the door, appeared a large snow leopard, the end of a broken chain dangling around its neck.

The gray leopard took a step toward them, its big teeth bared menacingly!

·10·

Double Dilemma

The twins stood frozen in place as the huge cat growled deeply, its teeth slick and shiny in the flickering candlelight.

"Listen!" Bert said, trying to keep his voice steady. "Don't scream, and do exactly as I say."

Just then, the leopard took another cautious step toward the children. They moved backward, too frightened to even open their mouths.

"He's used to being with humans," Bert went on. "He's as scared as we are. I want you to move slowly away from me.

G-go to other parts of the room and g-get to the door. But don't make any sudden m-movements!"

Despite his determination, Bert's knees began to shake. He knew that gamekeepers often controlled animals with their eyes, and he was praying inwardly that he would succeed in doing the same.

"What are you going to do?" Nan whispered.

"Freddie," Bert whispered back, "give me your camera, very slowly!"

Freddie pulled the strap over his head and, with trembling hands, placed the small box into Bert's outstretched hand.

"Everybody start moving," the older boy ordered.

Without another word, the Bobbseys inched away from their courageous brother, retreating farther into the antique-filled room.

Bert held the leopard's eyes, sensing the uncertainty in the animal. Apparently it had been in captivity for a long time and was looking toward Bert as if he were its keeper.

Nan, Freddie, and Flossie reached the door and began silently filing out. Bert lifted the camera to his chest, never taking his eyes from the creature in front of him. The cat followed the movement, and Bert clicked the shutter.

The flash flared brightly in the nearly dark room. It caught the leopard full in the face, blinding it temporarily. The animal turned around and around in a circle, roaring loudly.

Bert ran to the door and managed to get out before the cat was ready to attack him. He slammed the door behind him, then slumped against it, shaking with fear. After a few moments of heavy breathing, he regained his composure enough to walk over to Nan, who sat on a pile of ebony wood trying to comfort the smaller twins. They were crying.

"Hey, it's all right!" Bert exclaimed.

"I'm here and we're all safe."

"We . . . almost got eaten by that awful monster!" Freddie sobbed. "You w-w-were so brave, Bert."

"Aw, it wasn't that hard," Bert said with more conviction than he really felt. "That leopard was as tame as they come."

"We should have listened to Mrs. Wooley," Nan spoke up. "It was dangerous to come down here again."

Bert nodded ruefully and put an arm around Flossie, who was wiping her tears while she looked at her older brother admiringly.

"Well," the boy went on, "we found the wood and the missing animals. Now all we have to find is the man who took them."

"It was Denny Cole!" Flossie said. "Why won't you listen to me?"

Freddie pulled all his evidence photos out of his pocket again and spread them out on a board. Then he held the candle up over them. "I think Flossie is right. They look exactly alike," he said.

"But they couldn't be one and the same man," Nan pointed out. "One person cannot be in two places at the same time."

Suddenly Freddie jumped up, almost knocking the candle over. "They aren't the same man!" he cried. "I just noticed something that's different."

"What is it?" Nan and Flossie asked, crowding around their little brother. Bert stood above them, looking over their shoulders.

"The hair," Freddie said.

"I don't see . . ." Nan began, then she stopped. "That's it!" she exclaimed. "You're right. They part their hair on opposite sides!"

Bert started to laugh. "The solution is so simple and we great detectives never thought of it!"

Freddie joined in the laughter. "Those

men are twins," he bubbled. "Twins, just like us!"

"No, not like us!" Flossie objected fiercely. "They are bad, at least one of them is."

"Denny Cole wasn't very nice," Freddie said. "But it was his brother who stole your dollhouse."

"I have a feeling they're working together," Bert said. "One of them came to the hotel last night so we would see him. That way he could provide an alibi for his brother, who was robbing the zoo."

"You're right," Nan said. "I'll bet every time Denny stole something from the zoo, his brother showed up somewhere else, making sure he would be noticed by someone he knew."

"You're very clever!" a voice boomed angrily from the stairway.

The children whirled around to see Denny Cole, holding an electric lantern in his hand. Behind him stood a man who

looked exactly like him, only his hairstyle was different!

"Too clever for your own good," Denny went on, and both men stepped into the doorway, blocking the Bobbseys' only escape route. "And now we'll get rid of you troublemakers once and for all!"

11

Lost and Found

Denny set the lantern on a pile of ebony wood and folded his arms. "I'm the one you met at the airport," he went on with an evil grin.

"I knew it!" Flossie spoke up. "I knew you were, but no one believed me."

Denny Cole chuckled. "It doesn't matter now," he said. "You see, everything would have worked out just fine if you hadn't come along and stuck your noses into our business."

"It was our business, too," Flossie said steadfastly. "You stole my prize."

"And the wood our dad sent for the restoration!" Bert added.

"But why did you take the animals?" Nan inquired. She was hoping they could keep the men talking long enough for Mrs. Wooley to come back.

"That was my brother Danny's idea," Denny replied. "He and I were in prison for a robbery several years ago. There we met a man who had contacts with collectors of rare animals. He was willing to pay a good price for whatever we could supply."

"We hatched a plan," Danny continued. "And put it to work when we got out of jail. Denny went to work for the zoo, and whenever he took something, I'd make sure I was out where people could see me."

"And you'd pretend to be your brother," Bert added. "That way you always had an alibi."

"A perfect plan," Denny said. "When we were kids, we used to play around this old abandoned house. One day we discovered the secret room. Since no one knew about it but us, it seemed like the ideal spot to stash the animals while we arranged for shipment."

"But then the restoration project came along," Nan added.

Both men nodded.

"We were afraid our secret room would be discovered," Denny said. "So we stole the wood to stop work on the place."

"And when you heard about the dollhouse and the miniature," Nan spoke up, "you were worried that they also had a secret room, which might give somebody the idea to check the real mansion."

"Right," Danny admitted. "We tried to take the little one from your sister and ruin the secret room, but you interfered."

"What about the ghost noises?" Flossie asked.

Denny smiled a menacing smile. "We hadn't planned on that," he said. "When the animals make noise, the sound travels through the old central-heating system to the whole house."

"You'll never get away with this," Nan said.

Danny looked at his watch in the lantern light. "In about five minutes you'll be proven wrong," he said. "Our partner from jail will be showing up in a refitted milk truck to pay us and take the animals away. Then we'll take a plane out of the country, and live like kings."

"There's only one more thing we have to do," Denny said.

"Take care of the Bobbseys," Danny finished.

"You'd better not try anything," Bert told them. "The police are on their way here this very minute."

The men exchanged a look of disbelief. "We'll take our chances," Danny said. "Time is on our side."

"Yes, about fifteen years," came a voice from the stairs.

Everyone turned to see Detective

Wooley on the steps with his hands on his hips. He was flanked by several uniformed policemen.

"Did you hear it all?" Bert asked.

"We heard enough," John Wooley said, walking down the remaining stairs. He shook his head at the Cole twins as he snapped handcuffs on their wrists. "You should know better than to tangle with the famous Bobbseys."

A moment later, Janis Wooley and Mr. and Mrs. Bobbsey appeared. Greetings and hugs were exchanged all around.

"The missing animals are behind that door," Bert told Detective Wooley. "But you'd better call a zoo official. The snow leopard is loose."

"And here's my wood," Mr. Bobbsey exclaimed, patting a large stack. "And the tools, too!"

John Wooley laughed. "You kids sure made my job easy."

Flossie watched as the Cole brothers were led up the stairs. She moved to lean against a pile of wood, feeling a little sad. There was so much excitement in the room because everyone was happy. Everyone but Flossie.

Lowering her head, she looked at the floor. Suddenly she let out a squeal of delight. There, lying in a dark corner, was her little Gingerbread Manor!

She immediately ran to it. *Danny Cole must have tossed it over there after he stole it,* she thought, picking it up and checking for damage.

It was in perfect shape!

She hugged it close, delighted her little house was not broken.

The Bobbseys all filed out behind the police. The daylight outside seemed especially bright after the darkness of the secret room.

"How was your tour of Oklahoma City?" Nan asked her parents.

Mrs. Bobbsey laughed. "We thought it was pretty exciting until we heard what you've been up to."

Bert watched as the Coles were put into the back of a police car. He heard the noise of gravel crunching in the driveway and looked in that direction. A milk truck was screeching to a stop as its driver noticed the police cars.

Then it began to back up!

"It's the other thief!" Bert yelled, and ran toward the truck.

The driveway circled the front lawn. Bert cut across the yard and reached the street just as the milk truck was backing onto the main thoroughfare.

The truck had *Gilt Edge Farms* written on its sides and a commercial license on the back bumper. But before Bert could read the number, the vehicle sped away, kicking up a cloud of gravel from the edge of the drive!

12

Telltale Tire

Bert hurried back to Detective Wooley, who was running across the lawn to meet him. Breathing heavily, the boy told the detective what he had seen.

"Good work," the officer said. "But without that license number we may never get him."

Bert looked disappointed.

John Wooley put an arm around the boy. "You did the best you could."

After the Coles had been taken away, Mrs. Wooley took the Bobbseys back to their hotel in the station wagon.

"You'll probably have to go down to

the police station and make a statement later," she told them.

"I hope they catch that guy in the milk truck," Nan said. "I'd hate to see him go free."

"Do you think that was a real milk truck?" Mrs. Bobbsey asked.

"Gilt Edge is a local dairy," Janis replied. "It certainly looked like one of their trucks."

"There's one now!" Flossie said, pointing out the window. Parked by a restaurant on Lincoln Boulevard was a Gilt Edge truck!

"Maybe it's the one we're looking for!" Bert said excitedly.

Mrs. Wooley drove into the lot and stopped near the vehicle.

"That's not it," Freddie said with conviction.

"How do you know?" Bert asked. "It looks just like it."

"The tires are wrong," Freddie said, and held up a photo. "See?"

"You got a picture!" Nan exclaimed,

and examined it closely. "Why didn't you tell the police?"

Freddie shrugged. "I don't have the license number on it," he said. "Without that, I didn't think it was important."

They all leaned over to get a look at the photograph. The truck parked near the restaurant had white sidewalls on all tires. The truck in the photo had a blackwall tire on the left rear wheel.

"Too bad," Nan said, slumping back against the seat. "I thought we had something."

"Maybe we do," Bert spoke up, and everyone turned to him. "Look. Every policeman in Oklahoma City is doing the same thing we are right now—looking all over for milk trucks. The guy driving the one we're after must realize that, too. There's only one place where he could go and feel safe."

Nan sat up straight. "The parking lot at the dairy!" she exclaimed. "Let's get over there!"

"Not so fast," Mr. Bobbsey warned.

"That man is a dangerous criminal. We don't want to tackle him alone."

A man came out of the restaurant and climbed into the milk truck.

"Don't those trucks have CB radios in them?" Freddie asked.

"Yes," Nan said, opening her door. "We'll ask that man to call the police!"

She hurried out of the wagon and quickly explained their dilemma to the burly driver. He nodded, then came back to the car with her.

"My name's Ernie Crow," he introduced himself. "And I'll do anything I can to help. Come with me to the dairy. I'll call the police on the way!"

"Thanks," Mr. Bobbsey said. "We really appreciate it."

Janis Wooley followed Crow down Lincoln Boulevard to the south side of Oklahoma City.

"There it is!" Freddie said after a while, pointing to a huge sign that read *Gilt Edge Farms*.

Beside the sign was a low building,

with a huge parking lot filled with about fifty milk trucks.

Ernie Crow pulled into the fenced-in lot, while Mrs. Wooley parked on the street. The twins quickly jumped out of the station wagon.

"I'll stay here and wait for John!" Janis called, as the Bobbsey family ran toward the maze of trucks.

Ernie Crow waved to them. "Come on in!" he said. "I called and cleared you with the boss."

Hurriedly, they began checking the trucks, one after another, row after row.

Far down the end of the line, Freddie noticed a man sneaking around the back of a truck. It had a blackwall tire on the left rear wheel!

"There he is!" he called out.

The man looked up, saw the Bobbseys, and bolted for the employee parking lot.

The Bobbseys ran after him. However, they weren't quick enough. The suspect

got into a green Ford and it roared to life. He slammed it into gear and screeched through the lot, scattering the twins in all directions.

Just as he reached the gate, Mrs. Wooley pulled her station wagon in front of the exit, blocking it. The man skidded to a halt, unable to drive past her!

·13·

Gingerbread Manor

Seeing that his path was blocked, the man jumped out of his car and ran through the gate. Just then, five police cars appeared on the scene, blocking the whole street. The suspect was surrounded. Sheepishly, he put up his hands.

"You don't have anything on me!" he sneered as Officer Wooley approached him with a pair of handcuffs.

"How about stealing a commercial vehicle, flight to avoid prosecution, resisting arrest, and participating in the theft of valuable animals?" John Wooley said.

A policeman poked his head out of a nearby squad car. "The Ford he's been driving was stolen, too!"

"Rotten luck!" the suspect muttered. He glared at the Bobbseys. "Everything would have worked out just fine if you little snoops hadn't come around!"

Flossie shrugged. "If your friend hadn't taken my dollhouse at the airport, we wouldn't have suspected you. Now I'm glad he did!"

Nan squeezed her little sister's hand. "You're a real Sherlock Holmes, Floss!"

The next morning, Freddie proudly read the banner headline in the paper: *Young Detectives Solve Zoo Case.*

Beneath the heading were the pictures the boy had taken relating to the case— the airport photo, the smashed plexiglass around Gingerbread Manor, Denny Cole in the monkey cage, the secret room at the mansion containing the stolen wood, and the picture of the milk truck.

Flossie was just as happy about Freddie's contribution as he was. "You're an action reporter, Freddie," she said, hugging her brother.

Freddie grinned. "I'll take some more pictures at the celebration today. When are we leaving, Mom?"

"In a few minutes," Mrs. Bobbsey said. "As soon as Mrs. Wooley gets here."

When the family arrived at the Omniplex, they found it a beehive of activity. Gingerbread Manor was covered with a large sheet so that it could be properly unveiled before the large crowd that was gathering. On the first floor, Cherokee Indian dancers were performing in a roped-off section of the science display. They were dressed in colorful native garb, and their music was punctuated by drums and tinkling bells.

Flossie stood next to her twin brother,

staring at the miniature dollhouse in her hand. She loved her prize, and whether to leave it as a toy for the Flossie doll was a hard decision for her to make.

Mrs. Wooley looked at her watch. "We're ready to start," she said and tousled Flossie's hair. "Have you made up your mind yet?"

"No," Flossie answered in a tiny voice.

Janis smoothed her dress and hurried over to the dollhouse. The noisy onlookers became quiet.

"My friends," she said, "I want to thank you all for coming here today to dedicate Gingerbread Manor. This is the first act of the Centennial Celebration Commission.

"But, as all of you know, it's more than just an unveiling. We also wish to honor the Bobbsey family and the great contribution they've made to Oklahoma in the three short days since their arrival."

There was applause from the crowd.

"Let me begin," Janis went on, "by introducing you to Mr. Fiala, director of the Oklahoma City Zoo."

There was more applause as Mr. Fiala walked up to stand beside her.

"As a representative of all citizens of this fine state," he began, "I would like to thank the Bobbseys for solving the zoo thefts and for helping to bring the criminals to justice."

The applause grew so loud that it embarrassed the twins except for Freddie, who calmly snapped a picture of the zoo director.

Mr. Fiala continued. "By the power vested in me by the governor, I bestow on this wonderful Lakeport family the title of honorary citizens of Oklahoma, and I am making them lifetime members of the board of trustees of the Oklahoma City Zoo."

While the crowd clapped, Nan's thoughts drifted to the future. She knew she would be disappointed if there was never another mystery for the twins to

solve. Her fears, however, were un-
founded because before long the Bobbseys would be busy investigating the
Mystery of the Hindu Temple.

Nan was brought back to reality when
Mrs. Wooley took over. "And now the
moment comes that we've all been waiting for," she said, "namely, the unveiling of Gingerbread Manor!" She removed the sheet that covered the dollhouse.

The crowd gasped at its beauty. All the
rooms had been furnished, and its bright
colors were illuminated by a soft light
shining on it from the ceiling of the room.

This was Flossie's cue. She straight-
ened her shoulders and went up to Janis
Wooley, who introduced her. "Flossie
will now dedicate the Flossie Bobbsey
Room," she went on, "and unwrap the
Flossie Bobbsey Doll."

She handed the little girl a package she
had been carrying, and Flossie quickly

removed the brown paper. Then she gasped. Inside was a doll the height of a small pencil. It was dressed in play clothes and had a face exactly like hers!

A big smile came over Flossie's face as she held up the doll for everyone to see. Then she walked over to the Flossie Bobbsey Room and placed the doll inside. Next she put down her miniature dollhouse.

"Take good care of it," she said to the doll. "Play with it every day!"

The crowd cheered and applauded. Janis Wooley squeezed Flossie's hand. "You did it!" she whispered. "You really gave up your prize!"

Flossie nodded. "That's where it belongs," she said.